CORE LIBRARY OF US STATES

DELAWARE

BY HELEN EVANS WALSH

CONTENT CONSULTANT
The Education & Inspiration Team
Delaware Historical Society

Core Library

An Imprint of Abdo Publishing
abdobooks.com

abdobooks.com

Published by Abdo Publishing, a division of ABDO, PO Box 398166, Minneapolis, Minnesota 55439. Copyright © 2023 by Abdo Consulting Group, Inc. International copyrights reserved in all countries. No part of this book may be reproduced in any form without written permission from the publisher. Core Library™ is a trademark and logo of Abdo Publishing.

Printed in the United States of America, North Mankato, Minnesota.
052022
092022

Cover Photos: Shutterstock Images, (map and icons), (ladybug), (strawberry)
Interior Photos: Grindstone Media Group/Shutterstock Images, 4–5; Red Line Editorial, 8 (Delaware), 8 (USA); Stephen Furlong/Shutterstock Images, 12–13; iStockphoto, 15, 36–37; Carol M. Highsmith/Library of Congress, 18, 43; Shutterstock Images, 21 (flag), 21 (pie), 21 (crab), 21 (tree), 21 (fox); Nagel Photography/Shutterstock Images, 22; Khairil Azhar Junos/Shutterstock Images, 24–25, 45; KSC/NASA, 30–31; Linda Harms/Shutterstock Images, 32; Nick Raille/Shutterstock Images, 38; David Kay/Shutterstock Images, 41

Editor: Marie Pearson
Series Designer: Joshua Olson

Library of Congress Control Number: 2021951400

Publisher's Cataloging-in-Publication Data

Names: Evans Walsh, Helen, author.
Title: Delaware / by Helen Evans Walsh
Description: Minneapolis, Minnesota : Abdo Publishing, 2023 | Series: Core library of US states | Includes online resources and index.
Identifiers: ISBN 9781532197499 (lib. bdg.) | ISBN 9781098270254 (ebook)
Subjects: LCSH: U.S. states--Juvenile literature. | Northeastern States--Juvenile literature. | Delaware--History--Juvenile literature. | Physical geography--United States--Juvenile literature.
Classification: DDC 975.1--dc23

Population demographics broken down by race and ethnicity come from the 2019 census estimate. Population totals come from the 2020 census.

CONTENTS

CHAPTER ONE
The First State **4**

CHAPTER TWO
History of Delaware **12**

CHAPTER THREE
Geography and Climate **24**

CHAPTER FOUR
Resources and Economy **30**

CHAPTER FIVE
People and Places **36**

Important Dates **42**

Stop and Think **44**

Glossary **46**

Online Resources **47**

Learn More **47**

Index **48**

About the Author **48**

CHAPTER ONE

THE FIRST STATE

It's race day at Dover International Speedway. Fans arrive early at the track. Once the gates open, the crowds head inside the speedway to enjoy the races. From their seats, fans can see pit road. The race crews are hard at work. The race's grand marshal says, "Drivers, start your engines!" The NASCAR Cup Series race has begun. Dozens of cars speed around the track. Engines roar loudly as the drivers race lap after lap. After 399 laps, the final lap begins. The winning driver crosses the finish line, and fans cheer

Dover International Speedway is in central Delaware.

PERSPECTIVES

EARLY DAYS AT THE SPEEDWAY

The Dover International Speedway first opened its gates in 1969. Back then it was called Dover Downs. The track featured both horse and auto races. In the early days, it was hard to fill the stands. Denis McGlynn, president and CEO of Dover Motorsports, said, "It was pretty much a ghost-town atmosphere. We had 22,000 seats and we struggled to fill them." But by 2001 an estimated 135,000 people packed the stands on popular race weekends. Today attendance at the races has shrunk from its peak in the early 2000s. Speedway officials estimate about 45,000 fans visit the track on popular race weekends.

wildly in the stands. It's another race day at the speedway.

ABOUT DELAWARE

Delaware is a small state in the US region called the Mid-Atlantic region. Not everyone agrees which states are in this region, but most include Pennsylvania and Maryland. Mid-Atlantic states were some of the first places European colonists came to in the 1600s. Delaware is on the Delmarva Peninsula, which is surrounded by water. The peninsula gets its name from the three states that make up its land. Those states are Delaware, Maryland, and Virginia. Delaware is on the east side of the peninsula. It touches the Delaware River, Delaware Bay, and the Atlantic Ocean on the east. New Jersey lies across the river and bay. To the north Delaware borders Pennsylvania. Maryland forms the state's western and southern borders.

Delaware's nickname is the First State. In the 1770s Delaware was one of 13 American colonies. In the Revolutionary War (1775–1783), the colonies fought for and won independence from Great Britain. They became the United States. The leaders of the new country worked to create laws. They wrote the most important laws in a document called the Constitution of the United States. Delaware was the first state to ratify the US Constitution. For this reason it is considered the first state accepted into the United States.

MAP OF DELAWARE

Take a close look at this map. What roles do you think bodies of water have played in Delaware's history?

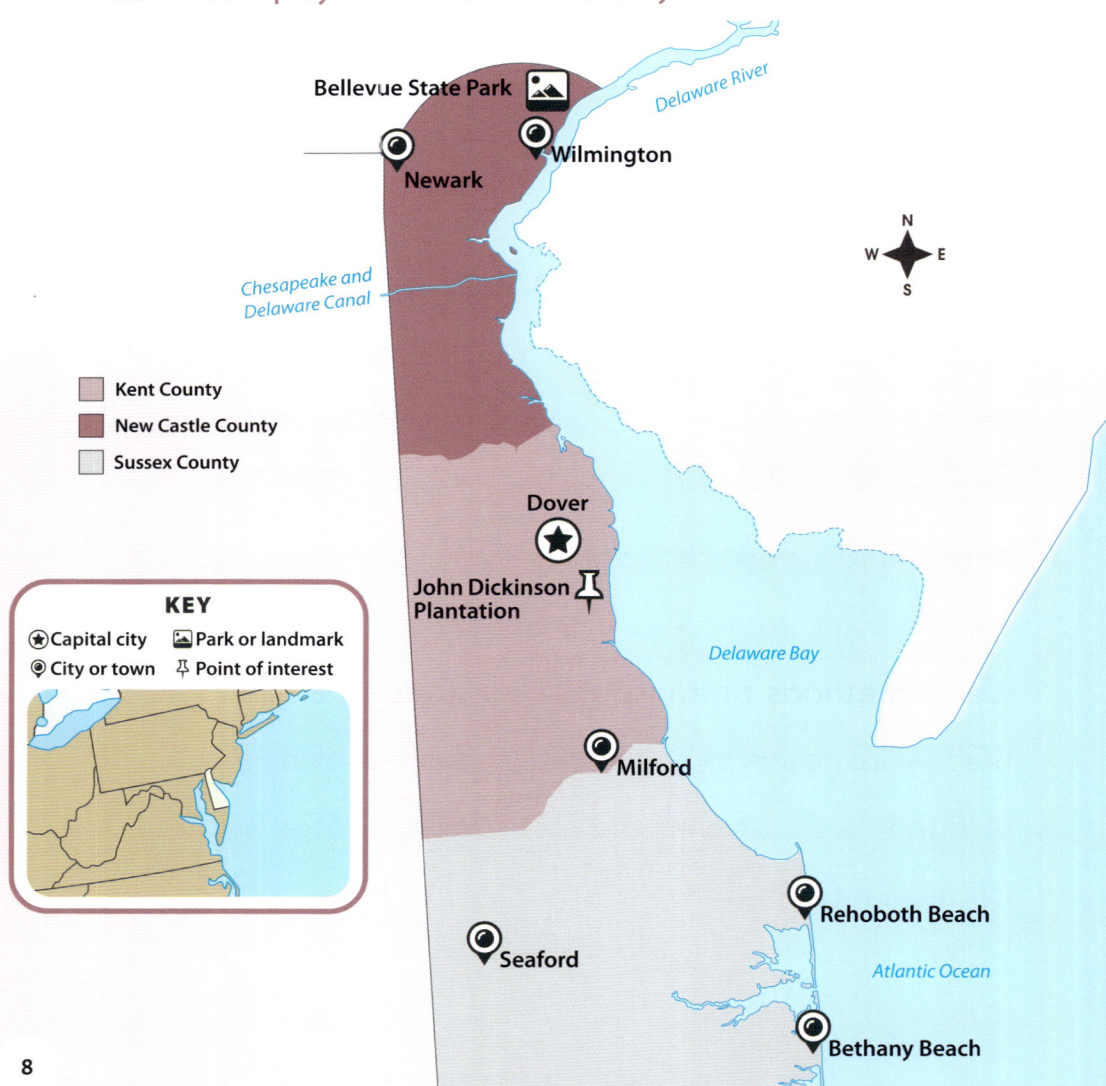

Delaware is divided into three counties, the fewest of any state. New Castle is the northern county. Kent County is in the middle. Sussex is the state's southern county.

Wilmington is Delaware's largest city. It is located in New Castle County. The city is built on the site of the first Swedish settlement in North America, Fort Christina. The Swedish purchased the land from the Lenape people. Today Wilmington is an important business and transportation center. The Port of Wilmington is the first major port on the Delaware River. Its location near the Atlantic Ocean makes it easy for ships to carry goods into and out of the country. From there railways and roads connect to nearby states. Products can be easily shipped to other states using these methods of transportation. Today many people visit Wilmington to see historic buildings and museums. Another popular site is the city's Riverfront, which has parks, shops, and restaurants.

THE DIAMOND STATE

Delaware is also known as the Diamond State. Thomas Jefferson may have given Delaware this nickname. He is said to have described Delaware as a "jewel" because of its important location along the East Coast.

Delaware's capital city is Dover. It is the second-largest city. Dover is located in Kent County. Most of Delaware's government business occurs in Dover. Like Wilmington, Dover offers city experiences such as museums and colleges. It is also home to the Dover International Speedway. Delaware has other smaller cities and towns, including Milford and Seaford.

In addition, the state has plenty of natural attractions. People enjoy outdoor activities in 17 state parks. They hunt and hike. They fish and boat on lakes, rivers, and the ocean. Delaware may be one of the smallest states, but it has a lot of places to explore.

STRAIGHT TO THE SOURCE

John Dickinson was raised in Delaware. In 1768 he wrote "The Liberty Song." It was his response to many colonists' outrage at taxes the British made them pay, even though the colonists had no elected representation in the British government. He wrote:

> *Then join Hand in Hand brave Americans all,*
> *By uniting we stand, by dividing we fall;*
> *In so righteous a cause let us hope to succeed,*
> *For Heaven approves of each generous Deed.*
>
> *All Ages shall speak with Amaze and Applause,*
> *Of the Courage we'll [show] in support of our laws;*
> *To die we can bear—but to serve we disdain,*
> *For Shame is to freedom more dreadful than pain.*

Source: "The Liberty Song." *Massachusetts Historical Society*, n.d., masshist.org. Accessed 14 July 2021.

WHAT'S THE BIG IDEA?

Read the above song lyrics carefully. What is the main point Dickinson is trying to make? Name two or three details he uses to support the main idea.

CHAPTER TWO

HISTORY OF DELAWARE

People have lived in Delaware for at least 12,000 years. The earliest people are now called Paleo-Indians. Eventually modern American Indian nations formed. By the 1600s the Lenape were the main people living in present-day Delaware. The Lenape name means "Original People." Their land is called Lenapehoking. They lived in the state's northern and central regions. Communities could have several hundred people. They fished the Delaware River. In the

Nanticoke people in Delaware continue to celebrate their culture. One way they do this is through dance and the arts at powwows.

summer they farmed. In the winter communities split into smaller family groups to hunt.

Other American Indian peoples also lived in Delaware. Several Algonquian-speaking tribes, including the Nanticoke, lived in the south. The Nanticoke name means "Tidewater People." The Nanticoke were farmers. They grew corn, beans, and other vegetables. They gathered berries and nuts, fished in nearby rivers, and hunted in forests. The Nanticoke lived in seasonal villages. They built dome-shaped homes called wigwams.

EUROPEANS ARRIVE

During the 1600s European settlers first arrived in Delaware. In 1610 explorer Samuel Argall named the Delaware River and Bay after Virginia's governor. His name was Thomas West, Lord De La Warr. The state of Delaware later took its name from the river and bay.

In 1638 the first Swedish and Finnish settlers arrived in Delaware. They named their landing site Fort

Christina became queen-elect at the age of five when her father, the king, died.

Christina after Queen Christina of Sweden. The settlers built farms and small settlements along the Delaware River. The colony was known as New Sweden. Most of the time, the Swedish and Finnish settlers lived peacefully with their Lenape and Nanticoke neighbors. In the 1650s the Dutch claimed the colony. It remained under Dutch rule until 1681. In that year, William Penn's

PERSPECTIVES

RECLAIMING THE LAND

Just outside Dover, Lenape Indian Tribe chief Dennis Coker's ancestors are buried in a small cemetery. Nearby is the site of the old Lenape schoolhouse. Now, Coker and the Lenape Indian Tribe hope to get some of this land back. They hope to preserve the historical landmarks and build a community center. "Right now, the Lenape Tribe of Delaware only owns one-half acre [0.2 ha] of a peninsula that we use to have had free roam of," Coker said in an interview. "As a sovereign nation of people we really need to be able to provide for ourselves, and we can't do that without land."

charter made Delaware an English colony and part of Pennsylvania.

As more Europeans arrived, they disrupted the hunting and farming of the Lenape and Nanticoke. When the Europeans cleared forests to build settlements, it greatly decreased the animal populations that the Lenape and Nanticoke hunted. The settlers complained that the Nanticoke tried to steal cattle and hogs from the settlements.

Conflict grew between the settlers and the Nanticoke and Lenape people.

In 1737 Pennsylvania leaders tricked the Lenape into the Walking Purchase. The Pennsylvania leaders pretended they had found a treaty from 1686. They told the Lenape their ancestors had signed the treaty. The treaty said that a portion of Lenape land now belonged to Pennsylvania. The Lenape did not want to go back on what they believed was the word of their ancestors. They lost a large portion of land. The Europeans forced the Lenape to move from present-day Delaware to land owned by the Haudenosaunee people. This led to fights between the Lenape and Haudenosaunee.

THE FIRST STATE

By the 1700s the British had 13 colonies, including Delaware, established along the East Coast. In 1776 the American colonies declared independence from the British. Delaware played an important role. Delegates from each colony voted for or against

A statue of Caesar Rodney was put up in Wilmington in 1923.

independence. Delaware delegate Caesar Rodney cast the vote that decided the colonies would go to war for independence. The colonists fought the British in the Revolutionary War. After defeating the British in 1783, they formed the United States. On December 7, 1787, Delaware became the young country's first official state.

Farming was very important to the state. People grew crops and raised livestock. But over time Delaware's economy changed. In the 1800s new factories opened in Delaware's northern regions. Many people moved to northern areas such as Wilmington to find work in factories.

In 1861 the American Civil War (1861–1865) began. Northern states, called the Union, largely did not agree with slavery. Southern states, or the Confederacy, wanted slavery to continue. Delaware was on the border between the northern and southern states. Although Delaware allowed slavery, it also had many free Black people. The state did not join the Southern states during the war. Delaware remained with the Union. Delaware's industry produced supplies for Northern soldiers. The DuPont company produced nearly half of all gunpowder used by the Union soldiers. Before and during the Civil War, Delaware played a role in the Underground Railroad. This secret network of people helped those who had escaped slavery head north to freedom.

After the Civil War ended, Delaware passed several Jim Crow laws. These were laws that denied people of color equal rights. They enforced segregation, or separation by race. These laws remained in effect into the mid-1900s. In the 1950s the civil rights movement

STUDYING STARS

Annie Jump Cannon was born in Delaware in 1863. She first developed an interest in stars when she was young. Cannon and her mother would lie on the roof of their Delaware home at night for fun. Cannon grew up to become a brilliant astronomer. She discovered hundreds of stars. She also invented a system to help classify stars. Her system is still used today. Cannon earned many honors for her scientific contributions. Additionally a crater on the moon is named after her. Cannon died in 1941.

grew and took hold across the country. People of all races protested segregation. Eventually the civil rights movement led to the removal of Jim Crow laws in Delaware and other states.

In that time the state's economy again changed. By the late 1800s, Delaware became a top producer of peaches in the United States. In 1875 the state produced 6 million baskets of peaches for sale. In the 1940s chemical and nylon manufacturing became a booming industry in Wilmington. By the mid-1900s poultry became another important agricultural product

DELAWARE
QUICK FACTS

Take a look at these facts and symbols of Delaware. How do you think each is important to the state?

State abbreviation: DE
Nickname: The First State
Motto: Liberty and independence
Date of statehood: December 7, 1787
Capital: Dover
Population: 989,948
Area: 2,489 square miles (6,446 sq km)

STATE SYMBOLS

State dessert
Peach pie

State tree
American holly

State marine animal
Horseshoe crab

State wildlife animal
Gray fox

Delaware's state capitol building is in Dover.

in the state. Farms often shipped poultry to nearby cities such as Philadelphia. Today Delaware's diverse economy has helped support many types of businesses.

STATE GOVERNMENT

Delaware's state government has three branches. The governor leads the executive branch. The governor works with the General Assembly, which is the state's legislative branch, to make laws. The General Assembly is made up of a Senate and a House of Representatives. The judicial branch is the state's court system.

The state of Delaware recognizes two American Indian tribes. They are the Lenape Indian Tribe of Delaware and the Nanticoke Indian Association. The Nanticoke have been trying to get federal recognition since the late 1900s.

FURTHER EVIDENCE

Chapter Two discusses the Lenape and the Walking Purchase. Identify one of the author's main points. What evidence does the author provide to support this point? The article at the website below also discusses the topic. Find a quote in this article that supports the author's main point. Does it offer a new piece of evidence?

THE WALKING PURCHASE
abdocorelibrary.com/delaware

CHAPTER THREE

GEOGRAPHY AND CLIMATE

Delaware is the second-smallest US state. It stretches 96 miles (154 km) long. It is just 35 miles (56 km) across at its widest point.

Delaware's land slopes downward from the hilly northern edge of the state, called the Piedmont region. Most of the rest of Delaware is flat and part of the Atlantic Coastal Plain. Most of Delaware's Coastal Plain has fertile soil. This soil works well for farming. Overall Delaware's land is low. In fact, Delaware is the

Bodies of water play an important part in many aspects of life in Delaware, including fishing.

25

second-lowest state in elevation. Only Florida has a lower average elevation.

DELAWARE'S WATERS

The state's main river is the Delaware River. The Delaware River flows from the northeast, forming the state's northeastern border. Some high and dry spots are found along the banks of the river. The river drains into the Delaware Bay. Marshes line the bay's shore. The bay flows into the Atlantic Ocean. Sandy ocean beaches cover land in the southeast. The state has 23 miles (37 km) of ocean shore.

The Delaware River is an important water source. Many people live near the river. The government protects it. About 50 percent of the surrounding land remains forested.

WEATHER

The weather in Delaware is moderate. That means the temperature does not get extremely hot or cold. The average daytime temperature in July is

74 degrees Fahrenheit (23°C). January is the coldest winter month. It averages 27 degrees Fahrenheit (−3°C). The weather often feels humid. Delaware gets about 45 inches (114 cm) of precipitation each year in the forms of rain and snow. The state can get heavy snowfalls in winter. Summer can bring severe thunderstorms.

PERSPECTIVES
CLIMATE CHANGE IN DELAWARE

All landforms and wildlife in Delaware are affected by climate change. Climate change is the overall warming of Earth's temperatures. It is caused by human activities such as burning fossil fuels. In Delaware more rainfall and hotter temperatures have been recorded as a result. This changes wildlife habitats. It can make survival harder for some species. Along the coasts, sea water levels are higher. Coastal flooding threatens the people and wildlife who live there.

Land near the Atlantic coast is affected by ocean temperatures. Usually the ocean keeps land slightly warmer in the winter and slightly cooler in the summer than inland areas.

HORSESHOE CRABS

Delaware Bay has more horseshoe crabs than anywhere in the world. The horseshoe crab is the state's marine animal. Delaware chose this crab because it is important in many ways. It is an essential part of the food chain. More than 1 million birds in the area feed on horseshoe crabs. The horseshoe crab's body also contains a substance used in medicines. Chitin, which is from the crabs' shells, is used to make bandages. Additionally the crab's eye structure is similar to that of a human's eye. Scientists study horseshoe crab eyes to help better understand human eyes.

PLANTS AND WILDLIFE

Despite the state's small size, thousands of plant and animal species live in Delaware. The state's varied habitats allow many species to live there. Plants and animals living in Delaware range from inland to coastal species. Hardwoods and holly trees are common in inland forests. Holly trees have thick, dark-green leaves and red berries. They can grow up to

60 feet (18 m) tall. Animals such as gray foxes, deer, and racoons live in wooded areas.

Moving toward the south, pines mix with hardwoods. Birds such as the sandpiper stop along marshes and coasts during migration. Goldenrod flowers pop up throughout the state. This plant with yellow blooms grows best near water.

EXPLORE ONLINE

Chapter Three discusses animals including the sandpiper. The article at the website below discusses shorebirds in more detail. Does the website answer any questions you had about animals in Delaware?

THE DELAWARE SHOREBIRD PROJECT
abdocorelibrary.com/delaware

CHAPTER
FOUR

RESOURCES AND ECONOMY

Delaware's economy can be divided into two main groups. Southern Delaware is by far the larger region. It is known for its agriculture. Northern Delaware is just a small portion of the state. It is known for business. A canal connects the Delaware River to the Chesapeake Bay west of the Delmarva Peninsula. This canal is called the Chesapeake and Delaware Canal. It makes it easier for ships to come and go from Baltimore, Maryland. The canal also

The astronauts of Apollo 11 wore spacesuits made from a material created by the Delaware company DuPont.

Many farms in Delaware raise poultry.

acts as a boundary between the state's northern and southern economies.

Agriculture has always been important in Delaware. Poultry is Delaware's main agricultural product. There are more chickens than people in the state. Corn, soybeans, and milk are the next most important. Vegetables are another key crop. People catch fish, crabs, and clams in the ocean and bay.

MANUFACTURING AND MORE

In northern Delaware manufacturing and business thrive. Factories in Delaware make many products. Manufactured items include chemical, food, paper, rubber, and metal products. Several large chemical companies, including DuPont, have labs and offices in Delaware. Finance and insurance companies bring in the most money for the state. The chemical and banking industries provide a large number of jobs.

Delaware attracts many top companies. The state is known for being business friendly. One reason many companies choose Delaware for headquarters is the Court of Chancery. This court specializes in dealing with large-business lawsuits.

THE CHEMICAL CAPITAL

Because so much chemical manufacturing takes place in the state, Delaware is sometimes called the Chemical Capital of the World. Chemical manufacturing includes pharmaceuticals, industrial chemicals, and plastics. DuPont is one of the world's top chemical manufacturing companies. DuPont scientists developed nylon, which has been used for many products such as pantyhose. The company also created the materials used to make the spacesuits worn by astronauts on Apollo 11. DuPont is based in Wilmington.

PERSPECTIVES

RETIRING

In recent years the number of retirees choosing to live in Delaware has increased. This is especially true in Sussex County. John and Bonnie Campbell moved from their home near Baltimore, Maryland, to southern Delaware when they retired. They were drawn by lower housing costs and lower taxes. "We actually like lower, slower, Delaware," John told *Delaware Online*. "We know who our neighbors are. Here, people make an effort."

Delaware is one of the few states with this type of court. Delaware also has low taxes and favorable laws for companies. In addition the state is in an accessible location for many people. The state is near several of the largest US cities. People can easily live in Delaware but work in New Jersey, Pennsylvania, or Washington, DC. This gives residents more options for jobs. In fact, President Joe Biden used to regularly commute on the train from his home in Wilmington to Washington, DC, when he was a senator.

STRAIGHT TO THE
SOURCE

In a 2013 interview, Ellen Kullman, DuPont's chief executive officer (CEO) and chair of the board, discussed the company's innovative history. She said:

> *Throughout the company's history, DuPont has created solutions through science that have solved big challenges, and we continue that tradition today. Our science is the engine that drives DuPont. Together with our partners, we are working with more people in more places than ever before to create transformative products and services that will help ensure a more secure food supply, find new energy sources and protect people where they work and live.*
>
> Source: "Interview with Ellen Kullman, Chair of the Board and CEO, Dupont." *ISO*, 28 Mar. 2013, iso.org. Accessed 4 Aug. 2021.

CONSIDER YOUR AUDIENCE

Adapt this passage for a different audience, such as your friends. Write a blog post conveying this same information for the new audience. How does your post differ from the original text and why?

CHAPTER FIVE

PEOPLE AND PLACES

With a small geographic size, Delaware's people are tightly packed. The state has one of the densest populations in the country. More than half of Delaware's people live in New Castle County. That is where Wilmington and many businesses are located.

Nearly 1 million people live in Delaware. White people who are not Hispanic or Latino make up 61.7 percent of the population. Black people make up 23.2 percent, and Hispanic and Latino people are 9.6 percent. Asians are

Wilmington is where many of Delaware's residents work.

Joe Biden was elected US president in 2020.

4.1 percent. American Indians, people of more than one race, and other populations are smaller percentages.

Famous people from Delaware include basketball player Elena Delle Donne, singer-songwriter George Thorogood, and jazz musician Clifford Brown. Actress Aubrey Plaza, who gained fame on the television show *Parks and Recreation*, is also from Delaware. Morgan Hurd is a gymnast from Delaware. In 2017 she was the women's gymnastics world champion. US president Joe Biden was born in Pennsylvania, but he and his family moved to Delaware when he was a child. He graduated from the University of Delaware and served as a politician for Delaware before being elected vice president in 2008.

PLACES

There is a lot to see and do in Delaware. Millions of visitors come to the state each year. Many people visit urban areas in the north for the region's major colleges, museums, and more. The University of Delaware is located in Newark. In Dover the Dover International Speedway draws racing fans. In Wilmington the Brandywine Zoo attracts animal lovers of all ages.

Delaware also offers a variety of museums. Visitors can view art at the Winterthur Museum, Garden, and Library. They can visit the John Dickinson Plantation to learn about one of

AN INVENTION WITH HUNDREDS OF USES

Stephanie Kwolek was a talented chemist in the 1900s. She worked at the DuPont factory in Wilmington. Kwolek is best known for inventing Kevlar. This material has more than 200 uses, including in bullet-proof vests. In 1994 Kwolek became the fourth woman inducted into the National Inventors Hall of Fame.

PERSPECTIVES

WELCOMING TOURISTS

Delaware has many attractions to offer visitors. In 2019 Delaware welcomed 9.2 million visitors to the state. Governor John Carney celebrated the number of tourists choosing to visit his state: "By supporting tourism, we also enhance the quality of life for all Delawareans by offering recreational and cultural activities and making sure there's even more cool stuff to do in Delaware."

the country's Founding Fathers and about the people who lived and worked there. Visitors can board the tall ship of Delaware, the *Kalmar Nyckel*, and learn about Delaware's maritime history. Other museums include the Delaware Art Museum and the Delaware Museum of Natural History.

Delaware also has many parks and nature preserves, including Bellevue State Park. People picnic, hike, fish, and explore at these places. At Cape Henlopen State Park, visitors can enjoy a view of the Harbor of Refuge Lighthouse. Many people vacation at Delaware's sandy beaches in the towns of Rehoboth Beach and

Some people enjoy paddleboarding along the shores of Bethany Beach.

Bethany Beach. They are known for their family-friendly activities and attractions.

From cities to small towns, Delaware has a variety of places to visit. People can enjoy indoor locations such as restaurants and museums, or they can enjoy the outdoors, including parks and the ocean. Delaware is full of adventure for everyone.

IMPORTANT DATES

12,000 years ago
Paleo-Indians begin living in what is now Delaware.

1600s CE
Multiple American Indian peoples, including the Lenape and Nanticoke, live in what is now Delaware.

1638
The first Swedish and Finnish settlers come to the Delaware region.

1737
Pennsylvania leaders trick the Lenape people in the Walking Purchase.

1783
The US colonies win independence from Great Britain and become their own country.

1787
Delaware becomes the first US state on December 7.

1875
Delaware produces 6 million baskets of peaches for sale.

1940s
Chemical and nylon manufacturing booms in Wilmington.

2020
Delaware politician Joe Biden is elected US president.

STOP AND
THINK

Another View

This book talks about the state of Delaware. As you know, every source is different. Ask a librarian or another adult to help you find another source about Delaware. Write a short essay comparing and contrasting the new source's point of view with that of this book's author. What is the point of view of each author? How are they similar and why? How are they different and why?

Say What?

Studying a state's history, geography, climate, economy, and more can mean learning a lot of new vocabulary. Find five words in this book you've never heard before. Use a dictionary to find out what they mean. Then write the meanings in your own words and use each word in a new sentence.

You Are There

This book discusses race day at Dover International Speedway. Imagine you are going to your first race at the speedway. Write a letter home telling your friends about your experience. What did you see and hear on the visit? Be sure to add plenty of detail to your notes.

Take a Stand

Some people move to southern Delaware, where towns are smaller and the pace of life is slower than in a big city. Others prefer Delaware's cities, where there are a lot of activities close by. Would you prefer living in a smaller town or a big city? Why?

GLOSSARY

charter
a document that guarantees certain rights and freedoms

classify
to arrange into a category or group based on shared characteristics

colony
an area of land that is separate from but controlled by another country

constitution
a document laying out the basic beliefs and laws of a nation or state

delegate
a person representing others

elevation
the height above sea level

fertile
rich in nutrients for growing plants

migration
the act of moving to a different location, usually as the seasons change

pharmaceutical
a medicine or drug

ratify
to sign or give formal consent to an agreement or document

ONLINE RESOURCES

To learn more about Delaware, visit our free resource websites below.

Visit **abdocorelibrary.com** or scan this QR code for free Common Core resources for teachers and students, including vetted activities, multimedia, and booklinks, for deeper subject comprehension.

Visit **abdobooklinks.com** or scan this QR code for free additional online weblinks for further learning. These links are routinely monitored and updated to provide the most current information available.

LEARN MORE

Gormley, Beatrice. *Joe Biden*. Aladdin, 2021.

Yasuda, Anita. *Traditional Stories of the Northeast Nations*. Abdo, 2018.

INDEX

agriculture, 14–16, 18, 20, 22, 25, 31–32
American Indians, 9, 13–17, 23, 38
animals, 16, 21, 28–29, 39

Bethany Beach, 8, 41

Cannon, Annie Jump, 20
Carney, John, 40
Chesapeake and Delaware Canal, 8, 31
civil rights movement, 19–20
Coker, Dennis, 16

Delaware Bay, 7, 8, 14, 26, 28
Delaware River, 7, 8, 9, 13–15, 26, 31
Delmarva Peninsula, 6, 31
Dickinson, John, 8, 11, 40
Dover, 5, 6, 8, 10, 16, 21, 39
DuPont, 19, 33, 35, 39

Europeans, 6, 9, 14–17

famous people, 38

manufacturing, 20, 32–33
museums, 9–10, 39–41

Newark, 8, 39

parks, 8, 9, 10, 40–41
plants, 21, 28–29

Rehoboth Beach, 8, 40
Rodney, Caesar, 18

wars, 7, 18–19
weather, 26–27
Wilmington, 8, 9–10, 18, 20, 33, 34, 37, 39

About the Author

Helen Evans Walsh is the author of several books for young adults and children. She enjoys traveling around the United States and has visited the state of Delaware several times.

48